Mary Hooper knows more tha............................
makes a good story – she's had over six hundred
published in teenage and women's magazines such as
J17, and is the highly regarded author of over fifty
titles for young people, including *Best Friends, Worst
Luck*; *Mad About the Boy*; *The Boyfriend Trap*; and
the Letters to Liz series. She recently won the 2000
North-east Book Award for her teenage novel,
Megan. Mary has two grown-up children, Rowan and
Gemma, and lives in an old cottage in Hampshire.

Books by the same author

Letters to Liz: Nicki's Letter
Best Friends, Worst Luck
The Boyfriend Trap
Mad About the Boy
The Peculiar Power of Tabitha Brown

Letters to Liz: Jo's Letter

Mary Hooper

WALKER BOOKS

AND SUBSIDIARIES

LONDON • BOSTON • SYDNEY

First published 2002 by Walker Books Ltd
87 Vauxhall Walk, London SE11 5HJ

2 4 6 8 10 9 7 5 3 1

Text © 2002 Mary Hooper
Cover illustration © 2002 Rian Hughes
Cover design by Rian Hughes at Device

The right of Mary Hooper to be identified as author
of this work has been asserted by her in accordance
with the Copyright, Designs and Patents Act 1988

This book has been typeset in ITC Highlander Book

Printed and bound in Great Britain by J. H. Haynes & Co. Ltd.

British Library Cataloguing in Publication Data:
a catalogue record for this book
is available from the British Library

ISBN 0-7445-5987-1

Chapter One

Chapter One

Dear Liz,

I met this really fit bloke on holiday and we fell madly in love with each other. His name is Vince and he's got jet black hair and wears those cool oblong glasses. He's quite tall, and muscly, and his mum works for a designer label, so on holiday he wore some really trendy clothes: no greasy jeans or tatty trainers like some of the boys I know!

The problem is that we live hundreds of miles away from each other. He's in Cheshire and I'm down south, so all we can do is write to each other. Being a bloke, though, he doesn't like writing letters so I hardly ever hear from him. I think my mates are beginning to wonder if he really exists.

The thing is, Liz, I've made Vince into this sort of ideal boyfriend but...

I paused over my letter, chewing at the end of my pen, and then I heard someone charging up the stairs. I just had time to turn my writing-pad over and shove it to the back of the table before Zoe burst in on me, all long brown limbs and thick blonde hair.

There are four of us, all best mates: me, Zoe, Amber and Nicki, and we'd been going round together for ages – long before we'd started at the comprehensive. It was the ratty end of the summer holidays and we had to go back to school in a week's time.

"Your sister let me in," she said. "What are you up to? You look guilty."

I felt myself turning pink. To hide this I stood up and opened the window. "I was just writing to Vince," I lied, and smiled a dreamy smile which I'd been working on. "I try and write to him every day. I promised him I would."

"Get you!" she said.

She started looking at my copy of *Sue CQ*, which was the mag we couldn't wait to get our hands on every Thursday morning. *Sue CQ* was the one fixed spot in our lives. We tried the make-up tips, copied the fashion, cooked the occasional pizza from one of their recipes, ogled the lads on that week's poster and did the quizzes.

The letter I'd been writing was to *Dear Liz*, so the mag was open at her section – four pages of emotional, heartachy problems. We read these pages first, and either snorted or giggled or sighed over each problem according to what it was about.

To get Zoe's attention away from the problem pages (suppose she saw the pad there and realized I'd been writing?) I said, "I got a *gorgeous* letter from Vince this morning." I gazed out of the window into the distance. "He said he's counting every minute until we can be together again. He said every time he hears our song it takes him back to the last night."

"Whoo!" Zoe said. "Sounds like he's *really* up for you." She flopped down on my bed. "What are we doing today, then? Shall we go round for Amber?"

"She's not in," I replied, a bit miffed that she seemed to have dismissed Vince already. "She told me she's going shopping with Jamie today to buy him a birthday present."

"She's too good to him," Zoe said darkly. "She's always buying him stuff. I keep telling her it's *them* who are supposed to buy *us* stuff." She smirked. "Jake bought me a CD last week – I already had it but I didn't tell him."

"When we were on holiday Vince bought me those earrings." I pointed to where they sat in pride of place on my mirror. "Coral, I think he said they were. Real coral."

But Zoe wasn't listening. She had seen them before and anyway, she had any amount of earrings: coral, gold, silver – diamond, probably. Zoe had most things. She stretched out on my bed, hanging her head over the side so that her hair hung down, thick and glossy, a blonde waterfall almost reaching the floor. I glanced at my own hair in the mirror: thin, wiry and frizzy. Frizzy! I ironed it, glossed it, gelled it and slicked it to my head, but it still came out frizzy.

"I might dump Jake," she said.

"Just because he bought you a CD you already had?"

"Nah. Because he's boring. I want someone more

exciting. I want an A-list celebrity."

"Round here?" I said. "You'll be lucky."

"Oh, I don't mind leaving here to go and find someone," she said. "I'll go to London, New York ... wherever." She looked across at me, "I suppose you just want to go to – where is it that the gorgeous Vince lives?"

"Chester," I said.

"That doesn't sound much cop," she said. She sat up suddenly, swinging her hair back from her face. "Well, if Amber's not in, let's do something else. Let's go and get Nicki out of bed."

I nodded. I was keen to go out. Well, I didn't want her to start looking around and find the half-written letter.

Chapter Two

"I had the most brilliant time with Sam yesterday!" Nicki said. It was later that morning and we were sitting in her garden on a rug, trying to sunbathe. I say *trying* because her garden is tiny and has a wall all round, so the sun only gets to about a quarter of it. She and Zoe were struggling to get in the best spot.

"Oooh! Brilliant time, eh? What happened that was so good, we ask ourselves," said Zoe.

"I wasn't going to tell you any juicy bits!" Nicki said. "I was going to tell you about *before* that."

"Ah. Shame!" Zoe said. "I like juicy bits."

They started giggling and I joined in, trying to match them giggle for giggle. "D'you think boys talk about us?" I asked. "D'you think they talk to their mates about what they get up to?" I rolled my eyes. "I'd *die* if Vince told anyone about what *we* did!"

Zoe and Nicki were still laughing and didn't take quite as much notice of this as I would have liked, so I added, "Talk about X-rated!"

There was a moment's silence and I hoped they were wondering about what I'd said, thinking that I was a bit of a dark horse. I hoped they wouldn't ask what I meant by X-rated, though, because – well, just because...

They weren't thinking anything about me, though,

because Nicki said, "No, what it was – we went to his brother's club and they let me do some DJ-ing."

"Yeah? Fat Girl Nick!" Zoe said, and we all laughed again.

The sun went behind a cloud and Nicki sat up. She was really pretty: she had streaky curly hair and what I thought of as a pussy-cat face: slanty eyes, wide cheekbones, big smile. OK, cats don't smile, but if they could they'd look like Nicki.

"Have you seen *Sue CQ* today?" she asked.

Zoe and I both said we had.

"In *Letters to Liz*, did you see that one about a girl and her stepfather? Did you believe it?"

"Nah!" Zoe said. "All those letters are made up."

"Bet they're not," Nicki said immediately.

"That letter was probably from Cindy," I said. I was talking about a girl in our class at school. "She's always going on about her stepfather. Right pig, he sounds."

"*Are* those letters all made up, d'you think?" Nicki asked.

"I shouldn't think so," I said, and felt a trickle of sweat run down my back. Careful... "I saw an agony aunt on TV a while back and she said they get hundreds of letters. They don't have to make them up."

"Yeah, well, there must be some pretty sad people around," Zoe said. "People who write to magazines can't have any friends to talk to, can they?"

"I suppose not," Nicki said.

"But what about..." I swallowed. "I mean, what if these girls are writing because there are things they can't tell their friends. Sometimes there *are* things, aren't there, that..."

Zoe yawned widely as I was speaking and my voice just trailed away to nothing. That was the trouble – they never listened to me, never seemed interested in what I had to say. That was why I sometimes felt I had to say something really shocking to try and make them sit up.

Nicki was looking at Zoe and laughing. "You opened your mouth so wide when you yawned, I could see what you had for breakfast."

"Then you saw chocolate croissants and freshly squeezed orange juice," Zoe said.

I looked at her enviously. Her mum was rich and she lived in the biggest house and had the best things ever: the trendiest clothes, loads of CDs and all the make-up she ever wanted. She even had the best breakfasts.

"I had a piece of dry toast," Nicki said. "What about you, Jo?" I didn't reply and she clapped her hands in front of my face. "Joanna Richmond! Wake up!"

"Sorry," I said. "I was thinking of something else."

"Don't tell us – Vince!" Nicki said.

I swallowed and lifted my eyebrows in the way Zoe did, looking at them in what I hoped was a secretive and sexy way. "How did you guess?"

"Probably because you don't think about anything

else these days. Talk about being loved-up. You're obsessed by that guy!"

"It's because it's her first proper boyfriend," Zoe teased.

"He isn't!" I said hotly.

"Who else has there been, then?"

"Well, I..." I could feel my cheeks beginning to get warm again. "It was before I was going round with you lot. I've had a couple of boyfriends."

"Oooh! Bet you haven't!" Zoe said.

"Not like you, eh?" Nicki said to her.

Zoe shook her head and her hair swung from side to side, sleek and heavy. I watched enviously: I'd have given anything to have hair that *swished*. "Can I help it if I'm popular?" she said.

"Who've you got your claws into now, then?"

Zoe rubbed a little more suntan lotion over her nose. "Bit short at the moment. All the really fit guys are away."

"What about Mike?" Nicki asked. "What about Robin Ellis?"

"Yeah, OK," Zoe laughed.

"So, just the two, then?"

I looked from one to the other: they'd practically forgotten I was there. "I'm going to collect my holiday photos this afternoon!" I blurted out, and then could have kicked myself. Why had I said that?

"Haven't you got them developed yet?" Nicki asked. "You've missed *days* of ogling Vince!"

"I hadn't finished the film," I said weakly.

"Oooh, we're going to see him at last!" Zoe squealed in false excitement.

"Well, you will if any of them have come out." I raked my hand through my hair like Nicki did, but it got stuck in the frizz. "My sister took one of us by the pool but she's probably mucked it up – got our heads missing or something!"

The sun came out and Nicki and Zoe started giggling and pushing each other out of the way to get into the best position again. I decided to go home. I'd promised Mum I'd be back by lunch-time and anyway, I had that letter to finish.

Chapter Three

After lunch, I grabbed the pad with my letter on it. I read through what I'd written and then I picked up my pen and wrote:

Have you read all the above about Vince, Liz? Bet you believed me about him, didn't you? Yeah, I can sound pretty convincing when I want to.

I hesitated and then I bit my lip and added,

The thing is, though – he doesn't exist. I made him up to impress my mates. And that's the real problem.

After I'd written that I glanced over my shoulder, as if Zoe or Nicki or Amber might come in and see what I'd written. I went on:

At least, he does exist somewhere – there was a boy on holiday who looked like the one I've made up, but I don't know what his name was and he certainly never even looked in my direction. Who would? I'm small and chubby and my hair is like wire wool. I've never actually had a boyfriend in my life – not gone out with one or kissed one, not even at a party. Zoe had a party last year and we played games where you had to kiss someone as a forfeit. When I was outside the door, though, all the boys made excuses rather than have to kiss me.

The trouble is, I've invented him now and I've done a pretty good job of it. I bet even you believed me! I've invented him so well I've almost started to believe in him myself. I actually found myself looking out for the postman this morning and making up excuses for him not having written – like perhaps he'd been too busy with his holiday job?

I'm getting in deeper and deeper and don't know how to get out. What shall I do now? Move him to Australia? Kill him off? Let him die in a motorbike crash? I really wish I hadn't started it.

The telephone began to ring downstairs. There was no one else in to answer it – my mum had gone out shopping with my sister – so I carefully hid my writing-pad and went down.

It was Zoe and she was bored. "I haven't got anything to do!" she wailed. "Come into town with me."

"I would," I said, "but I'm broke. I haven't even got the bus fare."

"But you've got to go in anyway, haven't you? I thought you were going to collect your holiday snaps."

"Oh yeah," I gulped. "I forgot."

"Forgot Vince!" Zoe hooted. "I can't believe that!"

"Well, I thought ... thought I had some money and

then realized I'd spent it. I can't afford to pick the photos up now."

"I'll lend it to you. I'll pay your fare in, as well," Zoe said. I'll say that for her – she never minds shelling out for her friends. Sometimes, though, her friends don't want it...

I shook my head. "No, I couldn't."

"That's OK! It's what I'm here for," Zoe said. "And if I lend you the money to get the photos I'll be first to see the gorgeous Vince."

I gave a false, nervous laugh. "You probably won't think he's all that gorgeous. I mean, *I* do, but he might not be your..." I forgot what I was about to say and coughed to hide my confusion. "And anyway, the photos might not be very good."

"Well, I want to see him anyway," she said. "I'll be round in ten minutes!"

An hour later we were outside the chemist's, and I was opening the long glossy envelope containing the photographs and feeling sick. Once it was clear there were no pictures of Vince, I was going to play it by ear. I'd blame it on the film, say it was a new camera and I hadn't known how to use it properly, say they must have got lost...

"So where is he, then?" Zoe asked, peering over my shoulder as I riffled through the snaps.

I groaned. "No! I don't believe it! He's not in any of them." I gave an agonized scream. "None of the ones with him in have come out!"

"He *must* be in one of them," Zoe said. We crossed the road outside the chemist's and sat on the wall. "Let me have a look."

I sat down and handed her the packet, pretending to be grief-stricken. "It's not fair! I've been just *dying* to see these photos!"

She went through them. "None of them are much cop, are they? They're mostly of views, or your sister." She looked sideways at me. "It's funny that *they've* come out but not the ones of him. How many did you take?"

I shrugged. "Not many. I didn't meet him until the second week, see. And then – well, you don't like to keep asking to take photos, do you? It looks too keen." I gave a pout that I'd copied from her.

"Nothing turns a guy off faster than being too full-on, does it?"

Zoe went through the photographs again and stopped at one of them. "There's a group on the beach here. Is he in that?"

"Let me look." I studied a photo I'd taken of the view along the beach, which just happened to have a long shot of a group of boys playing volleyball. Fantastic, I thought. *Saved!*

I gave a scream of joy. "There he is!" I pointed at someone on the far side of the net, someone tall and dark-haired who I'd never seen in my life before, but who – by some lucky chance – just happened to be in my photo. "There's Vince!"

Zoe studied the photo intently. "Yeah, he looks fit."

"It's not very good of him," I said. "It's a bit blurred because he was moving around."

"That's what you do in volleyball," Zoe said. She looked at it again. "I thought you said he wore glasses?"

I swallowed. "He does," I said. "But he takes them off for volleyball or footie or whatever."

"Right."

My heart was thumping. Did she believe me? She seemed to be looking at me with a funny expression. Don't say she'd sussed me...

She suddenly slapped me on the back and stood up. "Come on then, girl. Let's go!"

I stowed the photographs carefully in my bag. "Where to?"

"I want some sparkly nail varnish and matching lipstick. And I want some new hair slides and I'm thinking purple trainers."

"I might look for a card for Vince," I said. "Just a silly one to let him know I'm thinking of him."

"When *aren't* you thinking of him," Zoe said. "You've got it bad, girl."

"I guess I have," I said, and gave an elaborate sigh. "I guess I have..."

Chapter Four

"There's Amber!" Zoe said as we came out of the shopping arcade. She lifted an arm that was draped with shopping bags and pointed ahead of us at Amber, who was standing on the town hall steps.

"She doesn't look very happy," I said.

She didn't. Her shoulders were hunched and her mouth was drooping at the corners as if she was going to burst into tears any minute.

"What's up, matey?" Zoe asked, going up and flinging an arm round her shoulders.

Amber sighed, pushing her long fringe out of her eyes. Her hair was a pretty, gingery gold – I often wondered if her mum and dad knew what colour it was going to be before they named her. "He hasn't turned up!" she said. "Jamie hasn't turned up."

"The pig!" said Zoe, while I made sympathetic noises.

"We were supposed to meet here at three o'clock," Amber said. She looked at her watch. "And it's nearly four now."

"You shouldn't have waited so long!" Zoe said. "Ten minutes max, me. If they're longer than that then it's their hard luck."

Amber smiled a bit sadly. "Bet no one's ever stood *you* up."

"They wouldn't dare!" Zoe said. "Start as you mean to go on, that's my motto."

"Vince has never done that to me," I said, and then as they both looked at me a bit oddly, added, "but then I suppose I wasn't with him for that long."

Zoe tugged at Amber's arm. "Come along with us now. You're not waiting any longer!"

"But he might have got delayed somewhere. Or had an accident."

"Yeah, and he might have got beamed up to the planet Zog. Come on! I'm not letting you stand here like a lump. An hour's enough for anyone."

"We were going to choose his birthday present," Amber said dolefully, allowing herself to be led away.

"That's extra money you've got to spend on you,

then," Zoe said. "Let's go and get a drink."

Amber took another look round the square.
"OK," she said. "But can we go to Townies?" This was
the coffee shop that was part of the town hall offices;
it had a window which looked down on the square.

"So you can keep looking out and see if he comes?
No way!" Zoe said. "If he arrives late and you're not
here, then it's his hard luck."

Amber didn't say anything – I guess she knew it
was no good trying to stand up to Zoe. The three of
us walked back along the high street and into
Beany's to get a drink.

"And another reason for coming with us – you can
be second to see the photograph of Vince," Zoe said
to Amber as we sat down.

She turned to me. "Have you just got one?" she asked. "Did he send it to you?"

I shook my head. "It was among my holiday snaps — Zoe just lent me the money to collect them."

"Mind you — blink and you miss him," Zoe said.

I got the packet of photos out of my bag and passed over the volleyball one. "Lush!" Amber said, and added immediately, "I thought you said he wore glasses."

I sipped my coffee, trying to remain cool. I hated this part. *Hated* it. "He takes them off to do sport," I said.

"Really?"

I felt myself going hot under the collar. *Did* people take off their glasses to do sport? I wasn't sure.

"Does he take them off to snog?" Zoe said, and as Amber and I both laughed, added, "Well, that's a sport, isn't it?" She looked at me. "*Does* he?"

"Course not," I said.

My smile got fixed. Did people take their glasses off to snog? How would I know? I caught sight of our three reflections in the plate-glass window: one head of thick golden hair, one of tumbled amber hair, and one of dark frizz. No, I didn't know if people took off their glasses to snog and I was probably never going to find out. More than likely I'd spend the rest of my life making up boyfriends and telling lies.

Amber got up saying she was going to buy us double choc brownies. When she came back with them, Zoe asked her exactly how long she'd been going out with Jamie.

"Two months and twenty-two days," she said. "It's the longest I've ever been out with anyone." She shook her head. "Mind you, half the time I don't know whether I'm going out with him or not. Like now, for instance. For all I know he's dumped me."

"I wouldn't have thought so – not before he's got his birthday present," Zoe said. "My record for going out with a boy is two weeks," she went on, "what about you, Jo?"

"I met Vince two weeks and three days ago," I said.

"That was in the hotel disco, wasn't it?"

I fixed my face into a dreamy expression. "No, on the beach. My deckchair collapsed and he came and put it up for me."

"You told us it was the disco – because you said he was wearing a white shirt and you could see his chest hair under the strobe lighting," Zoe said.

I shook my head. "That was the first night we went out," I said swallowing nervously. I was sure, pretty sure, that was how I'd told it.

"He didn't seem to have much chest hair in the photo," Zoe said. She raised her eyebrows questioningly.

"It's very fair," I said, my smile fixed and bright. I wanted to scream; how come she could remember all this stuff?

Zoe was silent for another moment and I held my breath, wondering what she was going to ask me next, but she didn't ask anything. Instead she said,

"I've been thinking – my mum's going away next weekend, so I thought I'd have a party. Something to cheer us up before we go back to school. A consolation party."

"Fantastic!" Amber and I said, and I started thinking about what to wear.

"But it's not going to be a free-for-all with loads of gatecrashers," Zoe went on. "It's going to be a proper party – like a dinner party, with food and everything. And everyone's got to bring a partner."

"Oh," I said. Where was I supposed to get a partner from?

"I'll bring Jamie," Amber said. "If I tell him well in advance, he might turn up."

"Can't I come without a partner?" I said. "Only it's

going to be a bit difficult getting Vince..."

"Why is it? He doesn't live that far away, does he?" Zoe said. "Where was it?"

"Chester," I said, and then got a chewed-up feeling in my stomach. Had I said Chester – or Cheshire – before? Was Chester in Cheshire?

But no one seemed to have noticed anything odd. "That's easy. I've got an auntie in Chester – she comes down on the coach. He can catch that and you can meet him at the coach station and then he can stay with you for the weekend."

"The lovers' reunion!" Amber said. "Dead exciting, that'll be. Wonder if you'll feel the same?"

I fixed my smile so that it felt as if it was glued onto my face. "Oh, I'm sure we will," I said.

Chapter Five

"OK, let's do this week's *Sue CQ* quiz," Zoe said. It was a couple of days later and the four of us were at her house – as her bedroom was the biggest and poshest we usually ended up there.

We'd already gone through the mag reading out the problems, having a laugh about the most embarrassing ones and screeching at some of the answers. I hadn't finished my own letter to Liz, let alone posted it. If I *had* been writing, though, I had a new worry now: *Zoe's party.* What was I going to do about that?

"What's this quiz about?" Amber asked.

"*Does he really love you?*" Zoe read out. "*Find out if he means what he says.*"

"Huh!" Nicki said. "You don't need to do a quiz for that, because in my experience they never *do* mean what they say. They just spin you a line."

"They can't all be spinning lines!" I protested. "Vince for instance. That last night on the beach he said..." Every eye turned to me and I felt myself going red. "He said he'd never met anyone like me before." I blinked and in my mind I saw Vince, his face rather blurred like the guy's face in the volleyball photo, standing on the beach, his arms around me tightly. I heard him saying the words, his voice rather husky and broken, and I almost heard my reply. I thought I'd probably said that I felt the same.

"You didn't believe him!" Zoe scoffed.

"They always say that," Amber said quietly.

I shrugged. Zoe got some paper and we did the quiz. I had to concentrate hard, because it was all about what he – the boy in your life – had said to you when, and why, and where you were at the time and all that. I had to pay attention to make sure that I didn't contradict myself. As it was, I felt that Zoe seemed to have a weird look on her face whenever I said anything about Vince. Did she know?

Everyone lies in those quizzes, though. I couldn't see that my lies were worse than anyone else's. By the time we'd finished, and added up our scores and not come to any real conclusions, we were all bored with it.

"OK, let's talk about my party," Zoe said. "I've told my mum and she says it's OK. Have you all asked the boys?" She looked at me hard. "Have you asked Vince yet?"

I shook my head. "I rang last night but he was out."

"But there won't be a problem, will there? Your mum won't mind if he stays with you for the weekend? OK," she looked at me from under her eyelashes, "you may have to rein in your passion and have separate bedrooms..."

"I dunno," I said, pulling a face.

"I thought you said your mum liked him."

"She does, but..."

"Well, if he can't stay with you he can stay here!"

Zoe waved her arms about airily. "We've got loads of bedrooms."

I nodded, thinking wildly: did I have a cousin I could ask who could pretend to be Vince? Was there a boy I knew that they hadn't met? Could I afford a male escort or something? *What was I going to do?*

Zoe started writing lists of food, and asked us what we were going to bring.

"Put me down for pizza," I said. And then I added, "I'll do a mushroom and red pepper one, because Vince is a veggie." I don't know why I said that; maybe I thought it would make him more interesting and New Age-ish.

"Is he?" Zoe asked. "You never told us that."

"I thought you had fillet steak that last night you

went out together," Nicki said.

"I had fillet steak. He had some sort of veggie goulash."

They were all looking at me again and I rambled on, cursing myself for starting it. "Yeah, fillet steak! God, I felt awful when I found out he was a veggie. He just sat looking at my steak and it was all bloody and I felt terrible! I couldn't eat a thing."

"He doesn't look like a veggie in that photo," Amber said. "He looks quite macho."

I swallowed. Why had I said he was a veggie? They thought it sounded drippy. But what the hell did it matter anyway seeing as he didn't exist?

"I phoned Jamie to ask him," Amber said, "but God knows whether he'll turn up or not. I've said, though, that if he doesn't come to this party then I'm never going to see him again." She gave a weak laugh. "Not that I see him much anyway."

"And why did he leave you hanging around for an hour the other day?" Zoe asked sternly.

Amber shrugged. "He said he'd had a late night and was too tired to get up."

"And I take it that he doesn't have a phone at home?" Nicki asked.

Amber just shrugged again, looking miserable.

Zoe wrote down a list of who was coming. Us four, of course, and Joy and Naomi from school, and six boys. "Twelve. Just the right number," Zoe said. "Six girls with six boyfriends."

We all smiled round at each other smugly: happy

to be part of an attractive, popular little set, all with boyfriends. Or so they thought.

I cleared my throat. "I hope Vince can come," I said. "He might be working that weekend, though."

Zoe chucked her mobile across the bed to me. "Ring him now!"

"Yes, go on," Nicki said.

I shook my head. "He's working today."

"Can't you ring him at work?" Nicki asked.

They all stared at me and I said, "He's in the greengrocer's and they do deliveries. He wouldn't be there."

"Well, call him tonight," Zoe commanded. As if to anticipate what I was going to say next she added, "And if he can't come next Saturday, I'll have to change the date. We all want to meet Vince, don't we, girls?"

"You bet!" they all said.

Later, Amber and I walked home from Zoe's together – she was supposed to be seeing Jamie that evening. We arrived at her house and were just lolling around outside saying goodbye when her brother came out, shouted hello and went into their garage.

Amber grinned. "I think Aidan fancies you," she said. "I've noticed that whenever you're around he appears out of nowhere."

I stared at her disbelievingly. Amber's brother was two years older than us – same ambery hair, freckles, quite fit. But I'd never ever thought...

"No way!" I said. "You're having a laugh."

She shook her head. "No. Really. He asked me last week if you were going out with anyone."

"What did you say?"

"I told him he should have spoken up earlier and he was too late; that you were madly in love with a guy you met on holiday."

"But ... I expect he's just messing around," I said. "What about the others?" I was wondering what guy, given the choice, would bypass the other two for me. "What about Zoe and Nicki?"

She laughed. "They'd be too much for him to cope with. Eat him for breakfast." She looked at me curiously. "But you wouldn't be interested, would you? I told Aidan that you never stop talking about Vince. That it's a love job."

I found myself nodding furiously. "Yeah. Course it is. I'm *mad* about Vince!"

"That's what I thought," said Amber.

Chapter Six

"Got in touch with him yet?" Zoe said, ringing me first thing the next morning. "And don't you dare say that he can't come!"

My heart sank. She wasn't going to give up, was she? "I tried to ring but he was out again."

"He's out a bit too much, if you ask me," Zoe said. "Got someone else, has he?"

"Of course not!" I felt myself going all hot and cold at the thought – and then I remembered: how could he have someone else when he didn't really exist?

"Look, I'll try and get in touch with him today," I said to Zoe.

"Do that," she said. "Because I need to know about numbers. I don't want an odd one out at the table – someone there without a boyfriend."

Downstairs, I could hear my mum pottering about. "Look, I've got to go," I said. "Mum's just called me down for breakfast."

"OK, but ring me later to tell me whether he's coming or not. And Jo – tell him we're all *dying* to meet him!"

"Right," I said.

I put the phone down, went back upstairs and flopped onto my bed. What was I going to do? How was I going to get out of it? If I just said he couldn't come then they'd *know* I'd been lying.

Zoe wasn't going to let it drop, that was certain. And if she was going to change the date to suit him, how could I get out of it? I could just anticipate all the questions she was going to ask from now until the day of the party: "What colour did you say his eyes were?" "What sort of music does he like?" "Were you actually with him when he bought those earrings?" and so on. *We have ways of finding out if you're lying...*

I picked up the pad containing the letter to Liz and put it down again. What could *she* do? And anyway, even if I finished it and posted it today, I'd never hear back from her in time for next Friday. I got up, tore the letter into little pieces and flushed it down the loo.

*   *   *

When I came out of the shower I heard voices downstairs, and Mum shouted up that Amber had come round for me. I put my head over the banisters.

"I was just going to the shops," Amber said, standing in our hall. "I wondered if you wanted a walk."

I said I would, and that I'd be a couple of minutes. Amber went into the kitchen to wait and I hauled on a pair of jeans and a T-shirt and went downstairs.

As soon as I got in the kitchen I knew that something had happened. There was a funny atmosphere and Mum was looking at me strangely.

"Ready to go?" I said to Amber.

"Don't you want some cereal first?" Mum asked.

And then she said, straight out, "I didn't know you met a boy on holiday. You didn't tell me anything about it."

My heart sank and I felt a churning sickness at the pit of my stomach.

Amber was looking embarrassed. "I ... er ... just asked your mum if she liked him. Liked Vince."

"That's his name, is it? So when did you sneak off with him, then?"

"I didn't sneak off with him, Mum!"

"Was he there with his family, or what?"

"He was there with a crowd of mates," I mumbled. This was the story that Amber knew.

"Not that awful lot? Like football hooligans, they were!"

"No, not them. Another crowd."

"I don't remember another crowd of boys there."

I wanted to scream and I also wanted to kill my mum, I really did. Why didn't she just realize what I'd done and shut up? "They were at the next hotel," I said. "I only saw him a few times." I made for the back door. "Coming?" I said to Amber urgently.

"But there wasn't another hotel for miles!" Mum said, as Amber stood up and reached under the table for her bag.

I didn't say anything to this and Mum repeated, "For miles... And I do think you might have told me about him. Did you sneak out of the bedroom at night or what? Did you tell your sister? Did she wake up and find you gone?"

I felt hot and ill and horrible. I opened the back door and looked at Mum pleadingly. "I'll tell you about it later," I said, and just bolted down the path.

As we walked along the road I was too embarrassed, too incredibly embarrassed to speak, and for a while Amber didn't say anything either. When she did, it was just about the shopping she had to get and to point out a new lime-green VW Beetle that went past.

I thought about various things to say – about mums being such a pain, or that I hadn't told my mum because I'd wanted to keep it a special secret or some rubbish like that, but nothing I thought of made sense. I was just going to get myself in deeper and deeper. And what was Zoe going to say when she heard? *"Funny your mum didn't know about*

Vince. I find that very strange. Don't you, girls?"

I was silent in the shop. Amber got what she wanted and we began to walk back.

As we neared my house she started walking more slowly. "About Zoe's party," she said, and I felt my stomach curling up into a tight little knot. This was it. She was going to tell me she knew that I'd made Vince up.

"I mean, it should be good, but I'm really worried about it."

I looked at her in surprise. "Why?"

"Because I can't rely on Jamie being there. I've got a horrible feeling that I'll be sitting there waiting for him, waiting and waiting, and he won't appear. There'll be a place set, and all the food on the table, and Zoe will get cross and I'll feel really stupid."

I nodded slowly. "Could be tricky," I said. "I mean, he's not exactly reliable, is he?"

"I was thinking last night that, well ... boyfriends aren't everything, are they?"

"No," I said cautiously.

"I mean, the way Zoe and Nicki go on – if you haven't got a boyfriend you might as well be dead. Lately, though, I've been thinking that I'd be better off without one. Without Jamie. All I do is worry about losing him. So if I didn't have him in the first place I wouldn't be worried all the time."

I thought about this. Without Vince, I wouldn't be worried all the time either.

"Sometimes," she said, "I feel I just want to be in

control of my own life again."

When she said that, it really stopped me in my tracks. It was exactly how I felt: as if things were getting out of control. More and more lies were being piled onto the original one until the whole shaky pack of cards was going to fall down around me and cover me up.

We reached my house and sat down on the wall outside and I thought about what I ought to do next. Could I actually tell her what I'd done? How much of a good friend was she? Could I trust her not to tell the other two?

Neither of us spoke for a while, I guess we were both thinking, and then Amber said, "I've got an idea. Why don't we make a pact?"

"What sort of a pact?"

"You're worried about Vince not coming to the party, aren't you?"

I nodded. She knew — of course she knew.

"And I'm worried about Jamie. So why don't we decide for ourselves now that they're not going to be at the party *because we don't want them there!* Why don't we give them the elbow. Tell them we never want to see them again and..."

"And?"

"And no questions asked," she added quietly.

I stared at her. Was I ready to give up Vince? Since I'd come back from holiday I'd been something I'd never been before — one of those popular, lucky girls with a boyfriend. I'd had someone to talk about, someone to sigh over, someone to pretend to be soppy about. And yet where was this relationship going to lead? To my downfall, that was where. I'd get in deeper and deeper and then they'd find out and I'd be an absolute laughing-stock all over the school and everywhere else.

"No questions asked," Amber said again. "Just ... let's ... do ... it."

"OK!" I said, suddenly making up my mind.

"I'm going home now to ring Jamie – and you go in and ring Vince."

I nodded. "I'll tell him that a long-distance relationship just doesn't work."

I couldn't quite look Amber in the eye when I said that. She knew the truth – I was sure she did – but if she was a good enough friend to pretend she didn't...

"We'll do that, and later on I'll come back for you and we'll go to Zoe's. We'll tell her that we're coming to her party on our own, without a boyfriend between us, and she can like it or lump it."

"Too right!" I said.

Amber gave me an encouraging grin and went off. She carried on towards her own house and I wondered if, when she got in, she'd tell her brother that we'd both decided to pack up our boyfriends. Maybe ... sometime ... something would come of that. Or maybe it wouldn't, but as long as the imaginary Vince was around I wasn't going to find out, was I?

I walked on, starting to compose a letter in my

head. Well, if I'd invented an imaginary boyfriend, the least he deserved was an imaginary letter giving him the elbow.

Dear Vince, I'd say. You came in handy for a while but in the end you caused too much aggro in my life. Boyfriends are all very well, but sometimes a girl just needs her mates, and having a boy around confuses things. I hope you won't take this too badly, Vince. It was OK while it lasted – but this is goodbye...

Find out what Amber, Jo, Nicki and Zoe get up to

in another book from the Letters to Liz series:

Nicki's Letter

(Turn the page to read the first chapter.)

Chapter One

"Nicki, look at that," Zoe said, touching the little gold necklace hanging on a display board in front of us. "Isn't it gorgeous!"

I nodded. "Wow!" I said longingly. "I'd love that."

Zoe and I were in Heavenly, a jeweller's in town. We were on our way to meet the other two of our foursome, Jo and Amber, in Beany's. We'd just stopped off for some window-shopping along the way.

The gold chain we were looking at was very thin and delicate, with about ten tiny sparkly stones.

"It would look great with your black top," Zoe said.

"Yeah, it would," I agreed.

We looked at the price tag. "Whew!" I said. "An arm and a leg job." I let it drop back onto its black velvet card, and moved along the counter. Zoe stayed where she was, staring at it intently.

After looking at some bracelets at the other end of the shop and not really seeing anything I liked – or more to the point, could afford – I called to Zoe and told her to get a move on.

"Just coming." Zoe gave me a funny smile, then followed me out of the shop. We walked down the road for a while, and then she started giggling.

"Did you like that necklace?" she asked.

I nodded. "Lush. But way too much money."

"But did you really like it?"

"Yeah, I said I did."

She stopped walking. "Because – surprise, surprise! – here it is!" She pulled a black velvet card out of her pocket and thrust the necklace at me. "Put it away quickly before anyone sees it."

I looked at her in amazement. "But how did you get it?" My jaw dropped. "You didn't...?"

She burst out laughing. "That's right," she said. "I nicked it! Took it from right under their noses."

"But why?" I asked.

That wasn't such a stupid question as it sounds, because Zoe has never needed to steal anything in her life – she gets everything she wants anyway.

I mean, as soon as we read about something new in any of the magazines – whether it's a trendy haircut, clothes, posh make-up or CDs or whatever – she gets it. Everything.

She's got a different life to the rest of us. We all live in ordinary places but her house is brand new and on what's called "a select development of executive homes". She hasn't got a dad around – it's her mum who makes the money. She's got some high-powered job working with popstars, doing their insurance or something. She flies all over the world and earns an absolute fortune.

And as if all that isn't enough for the rest of us to be jealous of, Zoe is not only pretty enough to be a model, with long legs and thick blonde hair, but she sails through school-work, too. She's only got to read a book once and she remembers it, while I have to read and struggle through, then read it all over again before it goes in.

"Why did I take it?" she said then. "Because I wanted to."

"But..."

"I could have bought it and given it to you but that would have been too easy." She grinned. "I felt like doing something a bit daring."

"No, really..." I began. I felt shocked and sort of squirmy inside. "I don't really ... I think you ought to keep it."

She pushed it away. "I nicked it for you. It's yours."

What was I supposed to say to this? I hesitated, and

then I put the necklace in my pocket pretty fast. "Thanks," I muttered.

I found I couldn't quite look her in the eye. I mean, I'd liked the necklace but there's no way I'd wanted her to steal it for me.

Stealing. God, my mum is really funny about that. Like she's the only person I know who checks her change in supermarkets and if she's given too much, gives it straight back. And when I once found a five pound note in the street she made me take it round to the police station. All this honesty stuff must have rubbed off on me, I guess. I mean, I don't even like being late back with my library books – how sad is that?

We were only ten minutes late meeting Jo and

Amber and though we started chatting about this and that – boys, mostly – my mind wasn't on it. All I could think about was the necklace in my pocket. It felt as if I was wearing a great big neon sign around my neck with an arrow pointing to my pocket and words saying: STOLEN GOODS HERE!

I don't think I would have said anything to the other two, but Zoe was bursting to tell.

"Show them what I got you!" she said as soon as there was a pause in the conversation about these two boys we liked. "Put it on!"

I looked over my shoulder for police, store detectives and so on, not really wanting to bring it out. It was obvious that it had been stolen: it wasn't in a shop bag, for a start, and it was still on its velvet backing card.

"Wow!" Jo said. "What's that for?"

"Early birthday present?" Amber asked.

Zoe shook her head. "Just a little something..." She was on a high, giggling and tossing back her hair, loving being the centre of attention. "See what I give my friends?"

I shoved it back in my pocket again and Jo and Amber looked at me, puzzled.

"Was it in the sale, then?" Amber asked.

"Tell them!" Zoe said to me.

I looked round again. "She nicked it," I said in a low voice.

"Wow!" Jo said, and Amber's eyes opened wide. "Really?"

"Really!" Zoe said. She looked at us challengingly.

"Why not? I tell you, I got a real big buzz when I walked out of the shop with that necklace in my pocket."

"But what if..." Amber began.

"I'll worry about *what ifs* when they happen," Zoe said. "In the meantime, I think I'll do it again!"

Jo's eyes were gleaming. "Wow!" she said. "You're a jewel thief."

"Yeah, I suppose I am," Zoe said, raking her hair back with her hand. "An international jewel thief!"

They all started giggling then, and after a while I joined in. Inside, though, I was dead worried. Was she going to do it again? Suppose she got caught? Suppose I got caught with her? I had three problems in one.

When I got home and saw my new copy of the

magazine, *Sue CQ*, I immediately thought about the problem page. Yeah, that was it. I'd write to Liz, the agony aunt. She had all the answers.